AF228560

TEEN CHALLENGES

SUBSTANCE ADDICTION

by Donna B. McKinney

CONTENT CONSULTANT

Abigail O. Akande, PhD, CRC
Assistant Professor, Rehabilitation and Human Services
Penn State University—Abington College

Essential Library
An Imprint of Abdo Publishing | abdobooks.com

ABDOBOOKS.COM

Published by Abdo Publishing, a division of ABDO, PO Box 398166, Minneapolis, Minnesota 55439. Copyright © 2022 by Abdo Consulting Group, Inc. International copyrights reserved in all countries. No part of this book may be reproduced in any form without written permission from the publisher. Essential Library™ is a trademark and logo of Abdo Publishing.

Printed in the United States of America, North Mankato, Minnesota.
102021
012022

Cover Photos: Shutterstock Images, foreground; Kenneth Johnathan/Shutterstock Images, background
Interior Photos: Alexander Gold/Shutterstock Images, 4; Syda Productions/Shutterstock Images, 6; Shutterstock Images, 9, 10, 37, 44, 46, 60, 67, 88, 93, 97; Diego Cervo/Shutterstock Images, 13; The Washington Post/Getty Images, 18; Red Line Editorial, 21; iStockphoto, 25; Chip Somodevilla/Getty Images News/Getty Images, 28; Aleksandr Yu/Shutterstock Images, 33; Kimberly Boyles/Shutterstock Images, 38; David Smart/Shutterstock Images, 48; PA Wire/URN:43089253/Press Association/AP Images, 52; Mark Lennihan/AP Images, 58; Boris Roessler/picture-alliance/dpa/AP Images, 65; Fiona Goodall/Getty Images News/Getty Images, 70; DEA/R. Dell'orbo/De Agostini/Getty Images, 72; Uli Deck/picture alliance/Getty Images, 74; Dimas Ardian/Bloomberg/Getty Images, 76; Chris Knight/The Patriot-News/AP Images, 81; Brett Phibbs/NZ Herald/AP Images, 83; Yakobchuk Viacheslav/Shutterstock Images, 85; Dragon Images/Shutterstock Images, 87; Daisy Daisy/Shutterstock Images, 95

Editor: Katharine Hale
Series Designer: Colleen McLaren

LIBRARY OF CONGRESS CONTROL NUMBER: 2021941245

PUBLISHER'S CATALOGING-IN-PUBLICATION DATA

Names: McKinney, Donna B., author.

Title: Substance addiction / by Donna B. McKinney

Description: Minneapolis, Minnesota : Abdo Publishing, 2022 | Series: Teen challenges | Includes online resources and index.

Identifiers: ISBN 9781532196300 (lib. bdg.) | ISBN 9781098218119 (ebook)

Subjects: LCSH: Substance addiction--Juvenile literature. | Teenagers--Substance use--Juvenile literature. | Teenagers--Drug use--Juvenile literature. | Teenagers--Alcohol use--Juvenile literature. | Substance abuse--Prevention--Juvenile literature.

Classification: DDC 616.86--dc23

CONTENTS

Some people feel pressure from friends or classmates to try marijuana or other drugs.

THE CHALLENGES OF SUBSTANCE ADDICTION

Val first smoked marijuana, or pot, in the summer after eighth grade. She was worried about going to high school in the fall and wondered how she would fit in with the older, popular kids. So when Val's neighbor, a sophomore, offered her a joint one summer night, she tried it. She liked the buzzy feeling it gave her, and suddenly she felt like she was fitting in with the older kids on her street.

When school started, Val enjoyed her classes, and she even made the honor roll for the first grading period. She joined the cross-country team, and the coach told her she had great potential. Val made new friends on the team, and she enjoyed the meets and daily afternoon practices.

But her friends who smoked pot were asking her to hang out with them too. So on Friday nights, she usually found herself with her neighborhood friends. Soon, smoking pot became more than just a Friday night thing to do. Val looked for those friends at the end of the school day. The smell of pot clung to Val's hair and

People who suffer from substance addiction can find their performance in academics and other activities slipping.

clothes, and she worried her parents might notice it. She also hoped they wouldn't notice her bloodshot eyes. She missed a couple of cross-country practices, and the coach asked her what was going on. Then her report card for the second grading period arrived, and her parents asked her why the As and Bs had slid to Cs and even a D.

How did everything get so messed up? Val woke up every morning feeling angry, like her life was spinning out of control. Val's coach noticed that she was struggling. When he saw her in the hallway at school one day, he said,

"Val, you're a great runner, but you haven't been giving your best effort at practice. Is something wrong? Would you like to talk?" Val nodded, unsure of what to say. She was ready to make changes, but she needed some help.

WHAT IS SUBSTANCE ADDICTION?

The US federal government's National Institute on Drug Abuse (NIDA) describes drug addiction as a "chronic, relapsing disorder characterized by compulsive drug seeking, continued use despite harmful consequences, and long-lasting changes in the brain. It is considered both a complex brain disorder and a mental illness."[1] This means a person uses a drug frequently over time, unable to stop even if the drug use is negatively affecting his or her life. The terms *drug* and *substance* are often used when talking about addiction. *Substance* can refer to any drugs or alcohol, including prescription drugs, illegal drugs, inhalants, or nicotine in cigarettes.

Substance addiction happens when people cannot control whether they use a certain substance. They feel like they need the substance. When a person first starts misusing drugs or alcohol, it is generally called substance abuse. Examples of substance abuse can include taking drugs prescribed to someone else, taking prescribed drugs at the wrong dosage, or taking drugs for the sole purpose of getting high. Over time, the person's dependence on the substance grows. The abuse can become substance addiction or substance use disorder. The *Diagnostic and Statistical Manual of Mental Disorders, Fifth Edition* (*DSM-5*) is a tool used by mental health and health-care professionals to diagnose mental disorders. Substance use disorders are included in the *DSM-5*. There are 11 possible symptoms of substance use disorders, including giving up activities because of substance use, increased tolerance to the substance, and withdrawal symptoms. Someone with two to three of the 11 symptoms would be classified as having a mild substance use disorder. Having four to five symptoms would be considered moderate. Six or more symptoms would be a severe case, also called addiction. According to substance abuse expert A. Thomas McLellan, PhD, "These criteria are likely to reduce the all-or-none thinking (i.e., addicted or not addicted) that has characterized clinical approaches in this field."[2] In other words, addiction is a spectrum.

In talking about substance addiction, there are some different terms used to describe how a person uses the substance. NIDA defines the terms this way: *Drug use* refers to the use of any illegal drugs. *Drug misuse* describes the unhealthy use of a prescription medicine or alcohol. *Addiction* refers to a person's "inability to control the impulse to use drugs even when there are negative consequences."[3] Addiction is considered a brain disorder.

Alcohol, nicotine, prescription drugs, and illegal drugs all can lead to substance abuse.

PHYSICAL VS. PSYCHOLOGICAL ADDICTION

There are two kinds of addiction. Physical addiction means a person has used the substance so much that the body is physically dependent on the substance. The substance has caused permanent changes in the brain. When someone is physically addicted to a substance, the person may experience withdrawal symptoms if she stops taking the substance. These symptoms can include shaking, confusion, insomnia, mood swings, depression, anxiety, hallucinations, nausea, and general feelings of discomfort. The symptoms are severe enough to encourage a person to

Caffeine is the most commonly used drug in the world. Withdrawal symptoms can include headaches and drowsiness.

keep using the substance in order to avoid the symptoms. Some legal substances, such as cigarettes and caffeine, can cause physical addiction.

People can also be psychologically addicted to a substance. This means they crave the substance and feel a powerful urge to use it, even though they know it is harmful. Many drugs give the user pleasurable feelings immediately after taking them because of the ways the drugs interact with the brain. Yet the longer-lasting effects on the body can be devastating. Because of those initial pleasurable feelings, users want the substance over and over again. Only some substances are physically addictive, but a person can become psychologically addicted to any substance. People can experience symptoms such as depression, anxiety, confusion, or insomnia when they try to stop using the substance.

Sometimes a person might drink or smoke, but only in certain social situations. These might include going to a party or being with certain people. It might feel like this kind of behavior is harmless, yet it is possible for these social behaviors to lead to addiction.

THE DANGERS OF SUBSTANCE ADDICTION

Substance addiction can have deadly consequences for a person's health. When people abuse drugs, they might experience symptoms ranging from changes in appetite to heart attack, stroke, or even death. Over time, substance addiction can lead to heart, liver, or lung diseases; mental disorders; or cancer.

William R. Kelly is a professor of sociology at the University of Texas at Austin. He describes the devastating impact of substance abuse, saying, "The public health consequences of substance abuse are staggering. There were over 70,000 drug overdose deaths in 2017, the majority due to opioids. This represents a doubling of drug-related deaths in just 10 years."[4] Opioids are a class of potent painkillers that have a high potential for addiction.

Besides the direct health effects, substance addiction impairs a person's judgement. It can lead people to engage in risky behaviors such as driving recklessly, having unprotected sex, or sharing contaminated needles and syringes. This can lead to contracting hepatitis or HIV/AIDS. For a woman who is pregnant, substance abuse can lead to health and developmental problems for the baby, including having a baby who is born dependent on drugs.

DRUGS AND THE BRAIN

The human brain works like a complex computer, and drugs can interfere with how it functions. Drugs affect a person's brain stem, which is the area that controls important activities such as breathing and heart rate. The brain's limbic system is also negatively affected by drugs. This system plays an important role in people's emotions and the ways they feel happiness. Drugs also affect the brain's cerebral cortex, which controls decision-making, planning, thinking, and problem-solving. With repeated drug use, the body learns to tolerate what the drug does to the brain. More of the drug is needed to produce the same effects. This can lead to addiction.

THE PREVALENCE OF SUBSTANCE ADDICTION

Substance addiction is a far-reaching problem affecting people, families, and communities around the world. Alcohol, marijuana, and nicotine are the most commonly used substances among US teenagers. The American Academy of

Child & Adolescent Psychiatry reports that the use of illegal drugs is rising, especially for young teenagers. Fourteen is the average age for a teenager's first use of marijuana. Kelly says, "There are over 22 million individuals in the US who have a substance abuse problem (including alcohol). At any given moment, there are about 4.5 million individuals who have a substance use disorder due to the abuse of illicit and prescription drugs."[5]

The Youth Risk Behavior Survey (YRBS) tracks a variety of health behaviors among high school students, ranging from diet and physical activity to sexual activity and drug and alcohol use. The US Centers for Disease

Control and Prevention (CDC) has given the survey to students in grades nine through 12 every other year since 1991. In the 2017 survey, 29.8 percent of students reported drinking alcohol in the month before the survey. The same survey showed that 19.8 percent of students said they had used marijuana during the past month. Asked about cocaine use, 4.8 percent of students said they had used cocaine at some point in their lives.[6] Because the YRBS tracks self-reported behaviors, the actual numbers are likely higher.

HOW SUBSTANCE ADDICTION STARTS

Most people do not just decide to start down a dangerous, slippery path toward addiction. A combination of factors increases a person's chances of becoming addicted to drugs or alcohol. These factors include genes, home life and family history, how early the person starts using drugs, and what kinds of drugs the person uses. For example, young people who live with parents who are addicted to alcohol or drugs are four times more likely to become addicted too.

Teens who are depressed or who struggle to fit in are more at risk for developing drug and alcohol problems than teens who do not struggle with these issues. Often a variety of factors combine to make addiction more likely or less likely. The Harvard Medical School website reports, "Why one person can have a drink or two each day and not become addicted to alcohol, whereas another becomes addicted, is a mystery. People with a tendency to become addicted to

SIGNS OF A SUBSTANCE ABUSE PROBLEM

If someone is concerned about whether a family member or friend might be using drugs, there are some signs to watch for. Trouble at school—such as frequent absences, lack of interest in activities, or falling grades—can be a sign. Physical health problems, such as sudden weight gain or loss, low energy, red eyes, slurred speech, tremors, or appearing spaced out, are also signs. Sudden changes in personality or behavior, such as mood swings, short temper, or apathy, could also indicate a drug abuse problem. Loss of interest in personal appearance, such as not caring about clothing or grooming, might be a sign. Being secretive about where he is going or whom he will be with could be another indicator. Money problems are another sign, such as when a person suddenly asks to borrow money without giving good reasons or when family members notice that money appears to have been stolen from the home.

one substance also have a tendency to become addicted to others."[8]

THE EFFECTS OF SUBSTANCE ADDICTION

People who are addicted to drugs or alcohol face numerous health problems and, in some cases, death. Besides health issues, people who abuse substances often cannot give their best efforts in school, at work, or to family. Substance abuse touches every area of a person's life.

Substance addiction can have a negative impact on the lives of people close to the user. Data combined from the 2009 to 2014 National Surveys on Drug Use and Health (NSDUH) showed that approximately one in eight children younger than age 17 lived in a home where at least one parent had a substance use disorder within the past year. Within these families, doctors see children experiencing medical, psychological, and behavioral problems connected to their family member's substance abuse.

Substance addiction also affects communities. It makes workers less productive and leads to higher costs in health care. Addiction can contribute to unplanned pregnancies, drug-related crime and violence, and stress in family relationships. When a person is addicted to drugs or alcohol, there is a ripple effect in which the person's family, friends, and community are all affected. Whether people are abusing drugs or alcohol themselves or living with family members who are abusing substances, there is help to be found. The challenge of substance addiction can be overcome.

WHAT IS A DRUG SCREENING?

A drug screening is a test to find out whether people have traces of drugs in their bodies. The most common kind of drug screening is a urine test, in which a person provides a urine sample to a health-care provider. By analyzing the urine sample, the health-care provider can determine whether the person tested has used specific drugs within recent days or weeks. This kind of test can screen for both illegal and prescription drugs. Drug screening is done for a variety of reasons. Some employers require job applicants or employees to be screened for drugs. Sports teams or the military might require a drug screening. Some schools conduct random drug tests as a way of discouraging drug use among students.

While the legal drinking age in the United States is 21, laws about enforcement vary by state.

CHAPTER TWO

ALCOHOL

Alcohol is a substance that is legal for adults, yet it can lead to addiction when it is abused. While the minimum legal drinking age in the United States is 21, meaning people under 21 generally cannot purchase or consume alcoholic beverages, alcohol addiction can be a problem for teens too. The CDC reports that alcohol is the most commonly abused drug among young people in the United States.

ALCOHOL ADDICTION

Many adults enjoy drinking alcohol in moderation. Yet for some people, alcohol can become an out-of-control problem. When people abuse alcohol to the point that they lose control over how often and how much they are drinking and that they struggle emotionally when they are not using alcohol, the medical diagnosis is called alcohol use disorder (AUD). AUD is a brain disease in which people use alcohol compulsively and cannot control their drinking. It is not just a problem among adults.

Hundreds of thousands of teens in the United States have AUD.

AUD is also called alcoholism. The World Health Organization (WHO) and the American Medical Association define alcoholism as "a chronic, progressive treatable disease in which a person has lost control over her or his drinking so that it is interfering with some vital area of her or his life such as family and friends or job and school or health."[1]

UNDERAGE DRINKING

In the United States, the legal age for purchasing alcoholic beverages is 21. Before the National Minimum Drinking Age Act of 1984 took effect, the legal age for buying alcohol varied from state to state. Since 1984, researchers have found evidence that setting the drinking age at 21 saved lives and improved health for young people. The states that raised their legal drinking age to 21 saw their number of motor vehicle crashes drop. Underage drinking is an ongoing problem. Research reveals that excessive drinking by people under the age of 21 contributes to more than 4,300 deaths each year.[2] States still can set their own laws regarding alcohol, and some states have exemptions for religious ceremonies, parental consent, and educational purposes such as culinary school.

PREVALENCE

The University of Michigan has conducted the Monitoring the Future (MTF) survey for several decades. This survey tracks teenagers' behaviors and attitudes. One of the questions it asks is whether a young person has had an alcoholic beverage in the

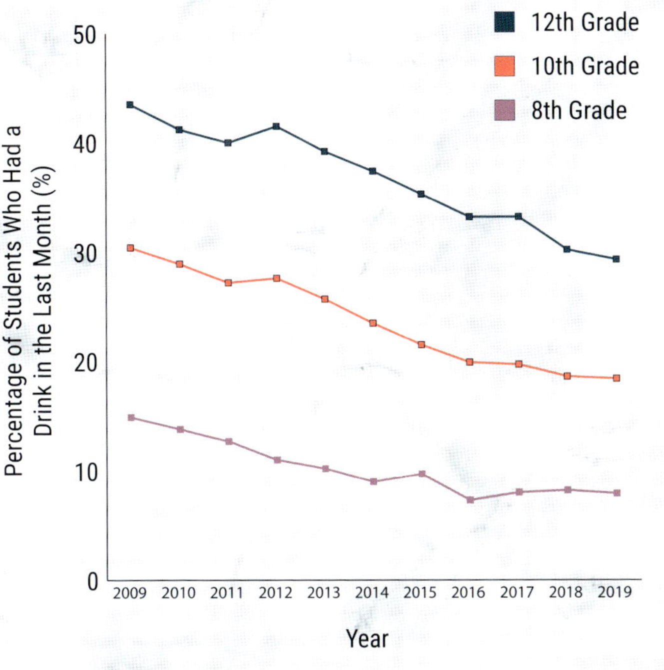

Alcohol use shrank among middle and high school students in the 2010s.

past 30 days. The 2019 edition of the study showed that 8 percent of eighth graders answered yes. The figure was 18 percent for sophomores and 29 percent for seniors.[3] Examining the study's findings over a long period of time shows alcohol use among teens declining. The study also shows that binge drinking among teens has dropped significantly since the mid-1990s.

Although the overall number of teenagers using alcohol is dropping, alcohol abuse can still be a major problem for some young people. The NSDUH questions people ages 12 and older about their drug use. The 2018 NSDUH showed that 2.3 percent of people ages 12 to 20 reported heavy alcohol use during the past month. While that percentage sounds low, it represents approximately 861,000 people.[5]

EFFECTS

In the United States, approximately 88,000 people die from alcohol consumption each year.[6] This makes alcohol the third leading preventable cause of death after tobacco and poor diet. For teenagers, alcohol abuse can be especially harmful because it interferes with healthy brain development and can also increase a young person's risk of developing AUD. The CDC states that people younger than 21 "should not drink any alcohol."[7]

Michael King took his first drink at age seven. By his teenage years he was addicted to alcohol. "It gave me all the confidence I'd never had. It made the bad times tolerable, and the good times even better," King explained. "But the thoughts of drinking and escaping never left my mind, and it became an obsession. I'd shoplift booze from the local convenience store, hide it from my family, and drinking alone became my regular getaway."[8]

The consequences of underage drinking are plentiful. Young people who drink can have problems in school, such as poor grades and absences. They may also engage in risky behavior, such as unprotected sexual activity, and underage drinkers have a higher risk for suicide than teens who do not drink. Underage drinking can disrupt a person's normal growth and sexual development. Alcohol can lead to problems with balance and reaction time. This can lead to car crashes, falls, burns, or drownings. Underage drinking can also cause memory problems. Young people who drink excessively can die from alcohol poisoning.

People who drink excessively also run the risk of developing long-term health problems. These include high blood pressure, heart disease, liver disease, kidney failure, digestive problems, a weakened immune system, and an increased risk for some cancers. Excessive drinking also increases a person's chances of developing mental health problems, such as depression or anxiety.

Families and communities experience the effects too. Some alcoholics seem to function well in daily living. Over time, however, excessive drinking can lead to problems in the workplace such as lost productivity and

ALCOHOL'S EFFECTS

Alcohol is classified as a depressant. This means that it affects a person's central nervous system by depressing, or slowing down, brain function. Slowed brain function results in a person having delayed reaction times, slurred speech, and poor coordination. However, even though alcohol is classified as a depressant, there are ways that it also acts like a stimulant in the human body. For example, a person who drinks alcohol may become more talkative, have an increased heart rate, and display overconfidence. The amount a person drinks affects whether the person experiences more of the depressant or stimulant effects of alcohol.

even unemployment. Within families, if a family member is drinking excessively, there is an increased risk of violence. Romantic relationships and parent-child relationships are affected in negative ways when a family member drinks to excess.

DANGERS OF BINGE DRINKING

One especially dangerous form of alcohol abuse is binge drinking. When people binge drink, they consume a large amount of alcohol in a short time period. The National Institutes of Health (NIH) define binge drinking as "drinking so much at once that your blood alcohol concentration (BAC) level is 0.08 percent or more."[10] BAC is a measure of how much alcohol is in a person's bloodstream.

Having a family member addicted to alcohol can lead to tension in relationships.

How long it takes to reach a BAC of 0.08 percent varies depending on body size. A man might reach this BAC with five drinks in two hours. A woman might reach this BAC with four drinks in the same period of time. Binge drinking is not rare. The 2018 NSDUH showed that approximately 11.4 percent of people ages 12 to 20 binge drank during the past month.[11]

Binge drinkers are more likely to kill someone, die by suicide, have a heart attack, get a sexually transmitted infection, drive a car under the influence, or be involved with the police, than someone who does not binge drink. Licensed professional counselor Raychelle Cassada Lohmann says, "Binge drinking is scary business. That powerful liquid has the ability to transform a life, and I don't mean in a good way. Intoxication can [wreak] havoc on a person's life and change it permanently, if not fatally."[12]

TREATMENT

For people who suffer from alcohol use disorder, formal treatment can include inpatient or outpatient treatment centers under the care of trained and licensed substance abuse treatment counselors. With inpatient treatment, a person enters a residential treatment program and lives there for a period of time while receiving treatment for the addiction. With outpatient treatment, the person attends treatment appointments and group meetings part-time while continuing to go to work or school.

"Rehab" is the short name often used to refer to any drug or alcohol rehabilitation treatment. The patient often goes through detoxification (known as "detox"), the process of getting drugs out of the body, when entering rehab. Because serious issues such as tremors, confusion, hallucinations, nausea, or vomiting can occur when a person addicted to alcohol stops drinking, alcohol detoxing should always take place under medical supervision. People should never try to detox on their own. Rehab treatment plans can include individual and group counseling, along with family therapy sessions. Therapists teach patients skills that will help them avoid going back to substance use after they leave rehab. People are not held at rehab against their wills, though friends and family may encourage them to attend. A person can also be required to go to treatment as part of a court sentencing. Sometimes therapists will have patients hospitalized for substance addiction, if the therapist fears the patients could harm themselves or others.

In addition to therapy, there are also medications that can help people who are trying to stop drinking. These include disulfiram, naltrexone, and acamprosate. Disulfiram works by creating unpleasant physical symptoms of nausea, vomiting, and headaches when a person drinks alcohol. Naltrexone works by blocking any good feelings the person gets from drinking, so the person loses the urge to drink. Acamprosate works by helping people fight cravings for alcohol once they stop drinking.

WHAT IS "ONE DRINK"?

The amount of alcohol in a drink varies depending on the kind of beverage it is. For example, beer usually contains about 5 percent alcohol, while hard liquors contain 40 percent alcohol. A standard drink is defined as the amount of a beverage that contains 14 grams of pure alcohol. A standard drink of beer is typically 12 ounces (355 mL). A standard drink of wine is typically only 5 ounces (148 mL). For hard liquors such as tequila, whiskey, rum, and vodka, a standard drink is only 1.5 ounces (44 mL). This means that if someone orders a mixed cocktail with three different shots of hard liquor, that "one drink" has the alcohol of three standard drinks.

Legislation to raise the national minimum age to purchase tobacco was first introduced in 2015 and was passed in 2019.

CHAPTER THREE

TOBACCO AND NICOTINE

Tobacco is another addictive substance that is legal for adults. In December 2019, the minimum age to legally purchase tobacco in the United States was raised from 18 to 21. This law includes all tobacco and nicotine products. But even though the law prohibits underage people from purchasing tobacco, many teenagers choose to smoke or use other tobacco and nicotine products. This can lead to addiction. According to the US National Cancer Institute, "The truth is, whether it's smoked, dipped, or rolled, any form of tobacco is harmful."[1]

TOBACCO AND NICOTINE ADDICTION

Tobacco is a plant whose leaves are harvested, dried, and turned into tobacco products, such as cigarettes, cigars, pipe tobacco, snuff, chewing tobacco, or hookah. What makes tobacco so addictive is an ingredient called nicotine. When a person smokes or uses other tobacco products, the nicotine gets into the user's body and changes the brain. These changes cause the person to become physically addicted to tobacco. Besides nicotine,

TOBACCO SPENDING

Tobacco companies spend billions of dollars every year trying to convince people to buy their products. But there are limits to the ways tobacco companies can advertise their products. In 1970, President Richard Nixon signed the Public Health Cigarette Smoking Act. It banned cigarette advertising from both television and radio. In 1984, tobacco companies were required to put US surgeon general warnings on all cigarette packs. In 1997, the advertising ban got stricter, prohibiting companies from advertising tobacco products outdoors, on billboards, and in public transportation.

tobacco smoke also contains other harmful chemicals, such as hydrogen cyanide, formaldehyde, lead, arsenic, and ammonia.

Nicotine is a stimulant. Once nicotine enters a person's bloodstream, it causes the adrenal glands to release a hormone called epinephrine, also known as adrenaline. This hormone causes the user's blood pressure, breathing, and heart rate to increase. Like ingredients in other drugs, such as cocaine and heroin, nicotine stimulates the brain's reward circuits and releases a chemical called dopamine. Dopamine is related to a person's feelings of reward and pleasure. Over time, nicotine use changes the brain, and the person becomes addicted as the body gets used to the heightened, artificial dopamine reward that nicotine produces. As a result, attempts to stop smoking can cause a person to become irritable, have trouble paying attention and sleeping, develop an increased appetite, and experience powerful cravings for tobacco.

ELECTRONIC CIGARETTES

Electronic cigarettes, or e-cigarettes, are battery-powered devices. They come in a variety of shapes and can look like regular cigarettes, USB flash drives, or pens. E-cigarettes create vapor instead of smoke. Because of this, using an e-cigarette is often called vaping. Though e-cigarettes do not contain tobacco, the vapor delivers nicotine and other harmful chemicals to the user's lungs. Like many other drugs, e-cigarettes are known by several different names, such as e-cigs, vape pens, vapes, e-hookahs, and mods. Besides being used for nicotine, e-cigarettes can also be used for marijuana and other drugs. The liquid vaporized by e-cigarettes used to be available in a variety of flavors, such as fruit and candy, that made them more appealing to

youths. In early 2020, the US Food and Drug Administration (FDA) banned production of flavors other than menthol and tobacco in an effort to curb teenage e-cigarette use.

PREVALENCE

Tobacco use is a widespread problem. The 2018 NSDUH
showed that 58.8 million people in the United States are
tobacco users. The survey showed that 47 million people
ages 12 and older have smoked cigarettes during the past
month.[3] Evidence also shows that e-cigarettes have been
increasing in popularity. According to the *Journal of the
American Medical Association*, approximately 10 percent
of high school students said they were using e-cigarettes
in 2016. By 2019, that number had risen to more than
25 percent.[4] Data from the 2018 National Youth Tobacco
Survey showed that from 2017 to 2018, e-cigarette use
among high school students increased by 78 percent, and
it increased by 49 percent among middle school students.[5]

EFFECTS

Long-term use of tobacco products can have deadly
results. The CDC reports that smoking cigarettes causes
more than 480,000 deaths in the United States each year.[6]
Tobacco use is the leading cause of preventable death in
the United States, contributing to lung cancer, respiratory
diseases, and heart disease. Scientists have also
connected smoking to leukemia, cataracts, type 2 diabetes,
and pneumonia. Millions of Americans live with a disease
caused by smoking cigarettes. Pregnant women who

Although teen use of regular cigarettes is declining, use of e-cigarettes is on the rise.

smoke increase their risk of having a miscarriage or a child born with low birth weight. Low birth weight contributes to a higher likelihood of developmental disabilities and sickness in infancy.

Diseases related to tobacco use also carry a financial cost. In the United States, smoking-related diseases cost more than $300 billion every year. Almost $170 billion of that amount goes to provide medical care for smokers. And $5.6 billion of the lost productivity is generated by people

SECONDHAND SMOKE

People who don't smoke might still be exposed to dangerous secondhand smoke. Breathing in that smoke is dangerous for anyone near the person who is smoking, especially for prolonged periods of time. Secondhand smoke carries harmful chemicals. It also increases a person's risk for lung cancer, obesity, and type 2 diabetes.

There is even a danger with thirdhand smoke. This is the residue of nicotine and other chemicals that tobacco smoke leaves on indoor surfaces, such as carpets, bedding, walls, clothes, and furniture. "Children and nonsmoking adults might be at risk of tobacco-related health problems when they inhale, swallow, or touch substances containing thirdhand smoke," explains Dr. J. Taylor Hays.[8]

People who do not smoke but are often around smokers can protect themselves. They can encourage family or friends who are trying to quit. People can also ask the smoker to move outside. As much as possible, people should move away from people who are smoking near them.

who are sick due to exposure to secondhand smoke, which is the smoke inhaled by people who are not smoking but are near smokers.[7] This means that people who do not smoke are suffering health problems because others are smoking.

In research funded by the US National Cancer Institute in 2011, scientists found that smoking begins to cause damage to the human body within minutes. Martin Dockrell, the director of policy and research at Action on Smoking and Health, said, "Almost everybody knows that smoking can cause lung cancer. The chilling thing about this research is that it shows just how early the very first stages of that process begin—not in 30 years but within 30 minutes of a single cigarette for every subject in the study. The process starts early but it is never too late to quit and the sooner you quit the sooner you start to reduce the harm."[9]

Some e-cigarette companies suggest that e-cigarettes are safer than traditional cigarettes, but this has not been proven true. The CDC states that because of the nicotine and other chemicals, e-cigarettes are unsafe for young people. NIDA seconds this, saying, "No matter what product it's in, nicotine is bad news."[10] Besides nicotine, there are other dangerous chemicals in e-cigarettes that a user inhales. Benzene, a compound found in car exhaust, is one of them. Heavy metals, such as nickel, tin, and lead, are all present in the aerosol from e-cigarettes. Another chemical is the flavoring diacetyl, which is linked to the lung disease bronchiolitis obliterans, commonly known as "popcorn lung." Popcorn lung causes scarring in the lungs that makes airways thicker and narrower, making it difficult to breathe.

VAPING DEATHS IN THE NEWS

In August 2019, health officials at the national, state, and local levels began investigating a nationwide outbreak of lung illnesses related to e-cigarette use. This outbreak was called E-cigarette, or Vaping, Product Use-Associated Lung Injury (EVALI). The CDC believes the lung illness is linked to vitamin E acetate, which is added to some e-cigarettes containing THC. THC, short for tetrahydrocannabinol, is the chemical in marijuana that produces a high. When vitamin E acetate is heated and inhaled, it can damage the lungs. While many THC e-cigarettes linked to EVALI were illegally sold on the black market, even some legal THC e-cigarettes were connected. EVALI symptoms include coughing, chest pains, trouble breathing, nausea, vomiting, diarrhea, fevers, chills, and weight loss.

Another risk with e-cigarettes involves defective batteries that have caused fires and explosions while the e-cigarette was charging. There is also some evidence that young people who use e-cigarettes might be more likely to move on to smoking regular cigarettes. Since modern e-cigarettes were only invented in 2003, doctors and researchers are still learning about their full impact on a person who uses them.

TREATMENT

Although nicotine creates a powerful addiction, people can have success in overcoming it. Behavioral treatments, such as self-help materials and counseling, can help a

Gum and patches containing nicotine can help people to quit smoking.

person fight tobacco and nicotine addiction. With these treatments, people learn to understand high-risk situations in which they might be tempted to use tobacco and then build strategies for dealing with those situations.

Nicotine replacement therapies are medicines approved by the FDA for help in fighting nicotine addiction. Nicotine replacement therapies give people a small, controlled dose of nicotine to help them through the withdrawal symptoms as they work to quit using nicotine products altogether. There are also some nonnicotine medicines that ease withdrawal symptoms. Medical professionals believe the most effective way to overcome tobacco addiction is by combining behavioral treatments and medication.

Marijuana can be consumed in many forms. Smoking, vaping, and eating edibles such as brownies or candy are all common.

CHAPTER FOUR

MARIJUANA

Most substances that can be abused are clearly either legal or illegal. With marijuana, this is not so simple. Marijuana's legality depends on where the user lives, why it's being used, and how it's being used. A number of states in the United States have legalized marijuana for recreational and medical use. In some states, marijuana is legal for medical use only. Yet in other states and on a federal level, marijuana is still illegal across the board. Whether it is used legally or illegally, marijuana abuse can cause problems for users. Common street names for marijuana include "pot," "weed," "reefer," "Mary Jane," and "grass."

Marijuana comes from the dried flowers, leaves, stems, and seeds of the cannabis plant. There are a number of ways people can use marijuana. It can be rolled into a cigarette called a joint and then smoked. Marijuana can also be smoked in pipes or bongs, which are water pipes. Some people even mix marijuana into food such as brownies or candy (commonly called "edibles"), or brew it as tea.

CBD

Cannabidiol (CBD) is an ingredient found in small amounts in the marijuana plant. CBD can also be derived from hemp plants. It does not cause a person to get high. Scientists have found some good uses for CBD. For example, it can treat seizures in children in the form of a medicine called Epidiolex. The FDA has given its approval for this medicine. Scientists are still studying CBD for possible use in treating other problems.

Some advertisers sell products such as oils, lotions, and even candies containing CBD. They claim that their products ease pain, help a person sleep, or reduce anxiety. More research is needed before scientists can confirm or refute these claims.

Marijuana contains a chemical called tetrahydrocannabinol (THC) that produces the high that users experience. THC is a mind-altering chemical. Marijuana is classified as a hallucinogen, and it is the most commonly used psychotropic drug in the United States. Psychotropic means that it affects a person's mental state—their mind, behavior, and emotions.

MARIJUANA USE DISORDER

Some people can become dependent on marijuana. This is called marijuana use disorder. If this dependence reaches a point that the user cannot stop using the drug despite its negative consequences on her or his life, it becomes addiction. The human brain adjusts to the large amount of marijuana a person is using. This makes it harder to stop. When people with marijuana use disorder want to quit using marijuana, they can experience withdrawal symptoms. These symptoms can include irritability, sleep problems, or decreased appetite. Other withdrawal symptoms can include restlessness, cravings, and various physical discomforts. These withdrawal symptoms can last up to two weeks.

Medical professionals report that 30 percent of people who use marijuana experience marijuana use disorder. The effect is greater for young people. Those who start using marijuana before age 18 are more

MEDICAL MARIJUANA

Marijuana used to treat illnesses is called medical marijuana. The FDA has not given its approval for the marijuana plant to be used as medicine. But the FDA has approved two medicines in pill form that contain cannabinoids, the chemicals found in marijuana. Cannabinoids provide pain relief, reduce anxiety, and relieve nausea. They can be helpful medicines for managing epileptic seizures and easing pain and inflammation. People who use medical marijuana can choose products with little or no THC in them. Medical researchers continue to study marijuana to see whether it could be useful in treating a range of symptoms related to medical conditions including HIV/AIDS, multiple sclerosis, mental disorders, pain, and addiction. Emergency room doctor Andrew Monte says, "Cannabis is not the root of all evil, nor is it the cure for all diseases. You've got to understand what the good is and what the bad is, and then make a balanced decision."[1]

likely to develop marijuana use disorder than adults who use marijuana.

PREVALENCE

In the 2018 NSDUH survey, approximately 43.5 million Americans ages 12 or older responded that they had used marijuana during the past year. This represents approximately 15.9 percent of the population. The same survey showed approximately 4.4 million people ages 12 or older had marijuana use disorder in the past year.[2]

The MTF survey also showed widespread marijuana use. This survey questions students in eighth, tenth, and twelfth grades. The study showed that marijuana use for students in those grades peaked in the 1990s and then began to decrease through the mid-2000s. But the 2019 survey showed a significant rise in daily use among students in eighth grade and tenth grade. Daily use is defined as using marijuana 20 or more times in the past month. The survey also noted a change in teenagers' attitudes toward marijuana use.

Since the mid-2000s, the number of teenagers who think regular marijuana use is risky has been dropping.

A newer way of using marijuana is with vaping devices. Users can vape THC. The MTF survey showed a rising popularity in vaping THC among teenagers. It was the second-largest increase in any drug use from one year to the next in the history of the survey.

EFFECTS

While some people might view marijuana as relatively harmless, it does have significant effects on people's health. "The biggest risk related to the use

HISTORY OF THE CANNABIS PLANT

In ancient cultures, the cannabis plant was used to make herbal medicines. Cannabis seeds have been found in graves in China and Siberia dating to around 500 BCE. In the United States, early European colonists grew hemp, another variety of the cannabis plant, to make their textiles. They used fibers from the hemp plant to make clothes, sails, paper, and rope. They used seeds as food. The hemp plants contained very low levels of THC, the chemical that creates the high that users experience. Recreational marijuana first became popular in the United States in the 1900s. Prohibition (1920–1933), a period in which the sale of alcohol was outlawed, and the Great Depression (1929–1939), a worldwide economic downturn, saw marijuana outlawed in some states. In 1937, the Marijuana Tax Act criminalized its use nationwide. Colorado and Washington were the first states to legalize recreational marijuana in 2012, and several other states have followed suit.

MARIJUANA LEGALIZATION IN THE UNITED STATES[5]

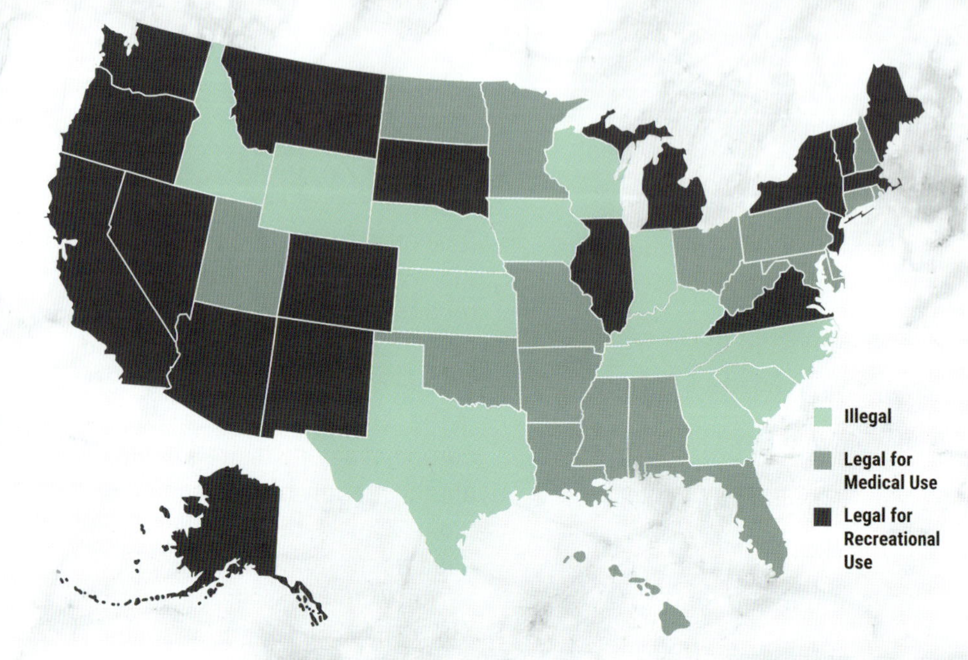

In August 2021, 18 states had legalized marijuana for recreational use.

of marijuana is the increased risk of psychosis," said Dr. Scott Krakower, the assistant unit chief of psychiatry at Zucker Hillside Hospital in New York.[4] Psychosis describes a mental disorder that causes a person to lose touch with the real world.

A study released in March 2020 showed that a single dose of THC found in marijuana (equal to one joint) can induce psychiatric symptoms. These can include symptoms of schizophrenia such as paranoia, which can cause people to think others are threatening them, and hallucinations. "The first takeaway is that for people in general there is a risk, even if you are healthy and taking a single dose, a one-off, you could have these symptoms," said Oliver Howes, a senior author on the study.[6]

Young people have even more to worry about. Using marijuana during the teenage years increases the likelihood that a person's IQ, a measure of intelligence, will drop. In a study of 1,000 people in New Zealand, researchers gave people IQ tests when they were age 13 and again at age 38. They tracked the people's drug use during that time period. The people who started using marijuana as teenagers and smoked it at least four times each week into adulthood saw an average IQ drop of 8 points.[7]

The 2018 NSDUH showed that marijuana use can cause significant health effects in young people and pregnant women. In pregnancy, marijuana use can harm the baby's health and cause problems such as stillbirth, premature birth, and developmental challenges. Marijuana use influences people's judgment and distorts their perceptions. Because marijuana use affects a person's cognitive abilities, such as coordination, vision, and attention span, it impairs driving. With long-term use, marijuana can contribute to memory impairment.

The federal government's Substance Abuse and Mental Health Services Administration reports that marijuana use affects how well people function in daily living. Those who

Many states have laws against driving under the influence of marijuana, though these laws are not as widespread as those against drunk driving.

use marijuana have a greater chance of having relationship problems. They do not achieve as well in school or their careers as those who do not use marijuana. Their satisfaction with life in general is lower than that of people who do not use marijuana.

TREATMENT

Studies have linked marijuana use to psychiatric disorders, such as schizophrenia, depression, and anxiety. However, more research is needed to determine whether marijuana use causes these conditions. Marijuana users might also be addicted to other substances, such as alcohol or other drugs. In these cases, health professionals often try to treat the underlying mental health issues first. This helps the person have better success in stopping the marijuana use.

There are no FDA-approved medications for treating marijuana use disorder, but scientists are researching possible medications. However, there are behavioral therapies that are successful in helping people overcome marijuana use disorder. These behavioral treatments include cognitive behavioral therapy (CBT), which helps people gain better self-control and stop drug use. Patients attending CBT work with a mental health professional to become aware of and change negative thinking, allowing patients to respond to challenging situations in a more effective way. Another behavioral therapy is contingency management therapy, which provides rewards when the person stays drug free. Patients might receive gift cards or cash prizes for negative drug-test results. This positive reinforcement can help rewire the reward center of the brain, replacing the need for drugs in order to feel rewarded.

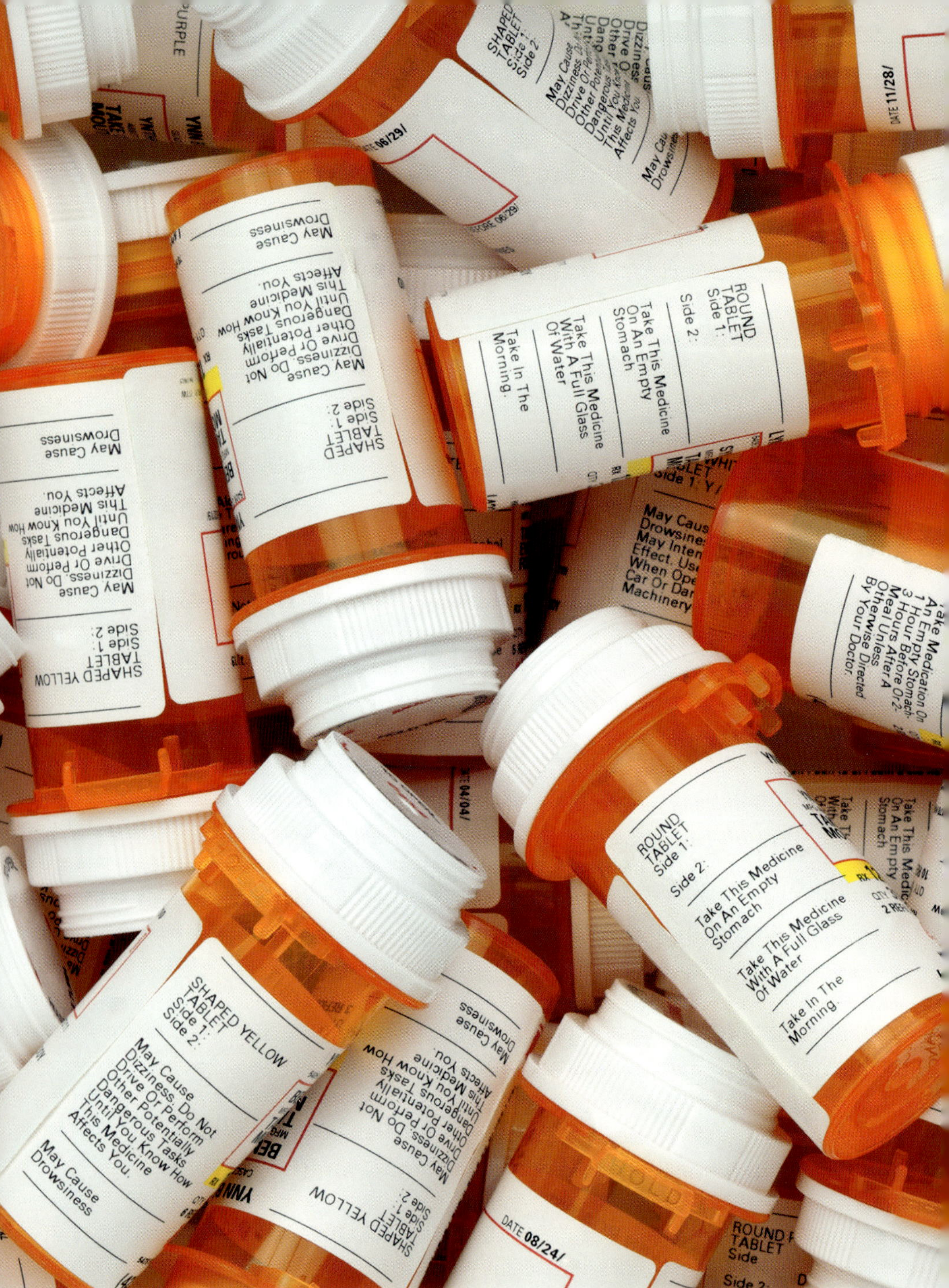

Prescription drugs are generally safe when taken as prescribed. But when people misuse them, they can become dangerous.

CHAPTER FIVE

PRESCRIPTION DRUGS

Sometimes substance addiction begins with a medicine that is beneficial when properly used, but when people misuse the medicine, it has the potential to become addictive. Prescription drug misuse happens when a person uses a medication in a way other than the way it is prescribed. A person might take someone else's prescription medicine. Or people might take their own medicine but at different doses than prescribed. They take the medicine in an attempt to get high. People can become physically addicted to prescription medicines.

Cortney was 16 years old when a friend gave her a prescription pain pill. "I went from being an honors student and varsity athlete to a high school dropout in just one year," Cortney said. "I tried to go to college after getting my GED, but my life revolved around using pills. I was so dependent on the pills that I became a shell of the person that I used to be." Cortney landed in jail before finally getting treatment for her addiction. She is now in recovery and working to help others seeking help to beat addictions. "Now, I work to let people know that no matter what you have done, there is so much life left to live."[1]

WHICH ARE ABUSED?

The prescription medicines most commonly abused can be divided into three groups. The first group includes opioids, which are used to treat pain. The second group includes central nervous system depressants, such as tranquilizers, sedatives, and hypnotics, which are used to treat anxiety and sleep problems. The third group includes the stimulants used to treat attention deficit hyperactivity disorder (ADHD).

Besides these three main groups, there is another category of prescription drugs that people abuse. These are appearance- and performance-enhancing drugs (APEDs). Anabolic steroids, also called steroids or androgens, are the most commonly abused APEDs. These are human-made drugs that imitate the male sex hormone testosterone. Doctors prescribe anabolic steroids to treat certain medical conditions, such as delayed puberty, loss of muscle related to disease, or low testosterone. But people abuse APEDs to increase their athletic performance or improve their physical appearance. Use of APEDs boosts the growth of people's muscles and also their development of male sexual characteristics, in all genders. Even though steroids do not produce a high, they are physically addictive for people who use them. Steroid users develop a tolerance, needing more and more of the drug to achieve the same effects. Users also experience withdrawal when they try to stop, with symptoms such as fatigue, cravings for the steroid, insomnia, restlessness, and reduced sex drive.

People who abuse prescription drugs get

STIMULANTS MISUSED FOR STUDY HABITS

ADHD is a disorder in which a person has trouble paying attention, is extremely active, and struggles to control impulsive behavior. For students who have been diagnosed with ADHD, prescription drugs such as Ritalin or Adderall can help them function better in all areas of life. However, some students who have not been diagnosed with ADHD use these stimulants in an effort to boost their academic performance. These teenagers believe that the drugs will help them focus better in class and during testing. Researchers have found that taking ADHD drugs such as Adderall and Ritalin does not help academic performance for teens who do not have ADHD. Teenagers who take prescription stimulants not prescribed for them run the risk of dangerous side effects such as increased heart rate and blood pressure, elevated blood sugar, seizures, psychosis, and paranoia.

Cyclist Lance Armstrong was stripped of his seven Tour de France titles in 2012 for using APEDs.

them from a variety of sources. Sometimes, it is their own medicine left over following a surgery. They take more of the medicine than is prescribed or continue to take it for longer than it is needed to treat the illness or pain. Sometimes a person who abuses prescription drugs takes another family member's prescription medicine. And some people who abuse prescription drugs buy them online without having a proper doctor's prescription.

PREVALENCE

Prescription drug addiction is a big problem in the United States. According to the US Department of Health and

Human Services, "The fastest-growing drug problem in the United States isn't cocaine, heroin, or methamphetamines. It is prescription drugs, and it is profoundly affecting the lives of teenagers."[3] Most misuse of opioids involves prescription pain medication. The more common prescription opioids include Vicodin, OxyContin, Percocet, and fentanyl. Heroin is an example of an illegal opioid. Once people become addicted to prescription opioids, they can easily turn to using street drugs such as heroin when their prescriptions end. Because opioid addiction can sometimes

DRUG TESTING IN ATHLETES

Sometimes professional athletes use anabolic steroids to strengthen their bodies and improve their performances in competition. This illegal practice is called doping. The World Anti-Doping Agency (WADA) was formed in 1999 to set anti-doping rules for sports organizations around the world. Sports organizations that do not control doping among their athletes face punishments, such as having events canceled or losing funding.

In the late 2010s, Russia became the center of an international doping investigation. The government had worked with its athletes to carry out a widespread doping program. The International Olympic Committee banned Russia from the 2018 Winter Olympics. Russian athletes could compete if they passed testing, but they had to compete under the title of "Olympic Athlete from Russia." In late 2019, WADA banned Russia from competing in international sports competitions for four years, including the Olympics and the World Cup.

start when a person has easy access to another family member's prescription medicine, it is important to handle prescription opioids properly. The American Medical Association recommends, "Treat your prescription pain medications like you would your jewelry, cash, or other valuables, which means keeping them in a secure place. Safe medication storage can mean keeping these prescription drugs under lock and key, if necessary."[4]

Steroids are less of a problem for teens, compared with other forms of substance addiction. The majority of people who misuse steroids are men in their twenties or thirties. Steroid use is less common among women.

EFFECTS

Prescription drug addiction has far-reaching and deadly consequences. Health-care professionals can see the growing problem of prescription drug addiction in the increases in emergency room trips, deaths by overdose, and people going into treatment programs. NIDA reports that overdose deaths caused by prescription opioids were five times higher in 2016 than in 1999.

Opioids affect the brain, causing nausea, drowsiness, constipation, and slowed breathing. Slowed breathing prevents oxygen from reaching the brain and other organs. This can lead to organ damage or even death. People who abuse prescription depressants can experience shallow breathing, fatigue, disorientation, slurred speech, and lack of coordination. When they try to stop using the depressants, they can experience seizures. People who abuse prescription stimulants can experience paranoia, irregular heartbeat, and a high body temperature.

For teenagers, the biggest danger in abusing prescription medicines is their effect on the still-developing brain. Parts of the human brain continue to develop until people reach their early to mid-twenties. These include the prefrontal cortex, which controls impulses, sets priorities, and focuses attention. Also developing is the brain's outer mantle, which helps people understand laws, rules, and social behavior. During the teenage years, addiction can be hardwired into a person's brain with lifelong consequences.

The abuse of opioids is a public health crisis in the United States. This crisis, including both prescription medicines and illegal opioids, does not discriminate. It affects the social, medical, and economic welfare

SUBSTANCE USE AND PREGNANCY

The drugs a mother uses during pregnancy are passed through the umbilical cord to the baby. According to NIDA, "Babies born to mothers who have problems with drugs aren't born addicted, but the babies can be born with drugs in their system."[7] What these babies experience is called neonatal abstinence syndrome (NAS). If a mother uses opioids during pregnancy, such as prescription pain medicines or heroin, babies may experience tremors, fever, or seizures. They may have trouble breathing or feeding after birth. Babies born with NAS usually need to stay in the hospital longer than babies born to drug-free mothers, and they require medicines to ease the discomfort caused by their mothers' drug use. These hospital stays in neonatal intensive care units are very expensive. Pregnant women who are addicted to opioids can get help. There are medicines that can be used to treat the addiction, helping both the baby and mother to get healthy.

of people across all socioeconomic levels, ethnicities, and occupations. Using 2013 data, the CDC put a price tag of $78.5 billion a year on the "economic burden" caused by opioid misuse.[6] This dollar amount includes costs of health care, lost productivity, addiction treatments, and the criminal justice impact.

Although the number of teenagers using steroids and other APEDs is relatively small, the health consequences can be severe. Steroid use can trigger aggressive behavior, called "roid rage," and wild mood swings. Long-term steroid use can cause stunted growth in teenagers, high blood pressure, heart attack, stroke, liver disease, or kidney failure. Steroid use can cause hormone imbalance. Among male users, this can cause breast growth, shrinking testicles, and baldness. Among female users, steroid use can cause growth of facial hair, a deepening voice, and baldness.

TREATMENT

The two main methods for treating prescription drug abuse are behavioral therapy, such as CBT and contingency management therapy, and medications. It may seem counterintuitive to treat prescription drug abuse with more medication. However, medicines such as buprenorphine, methadone, and extended-release naltrexone have proven to be effective in fighting opioid addiction.

MIXING MEDICATIONS

Sometimes people can overdose on drugs when they mix medicines that should not be taken at the same time. This can happen with both prescription medicines and over-the-counter medicines, which don't need a prescription. Every drug has an active ingredient that is intended to work a certain way within the body. When a person takes two medications at the same time, it can change the way the active ingredients work. These changes can sometimes have unexpected and even dangerous results. Medicines are labeled with instructions on doses and warnings about the way they interact with other drugs. A doctor or pharmacist can help answer questions a patient might have about the possible results of mixing two medicines.

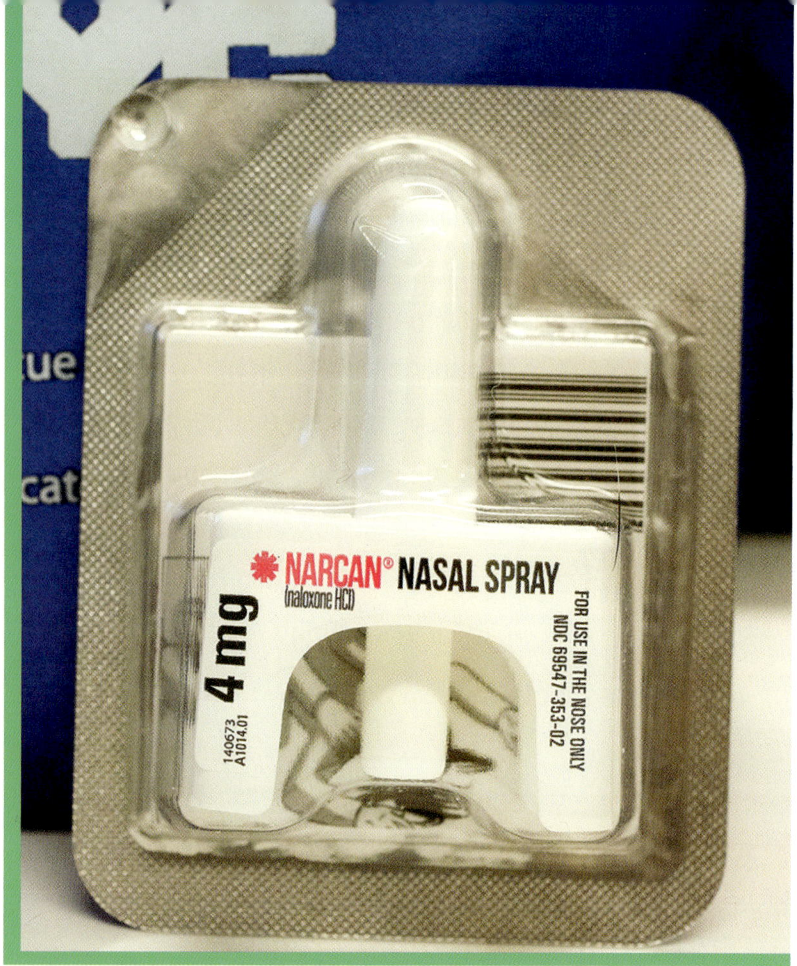

If administered in time, naloxone can help reverse an opioid overdose.

Some of these medicines keep opioids from affecting the brain, while others ease withdrawal symptoms. Besides these medications, scientists are also looking at new treatment options, such as vaccines that attack the opioids in a person's bloodstream so they do not reach the brain.

There is another medicine called naloxone that can be administered to reverse the effects of an overdose. Narcan and Evzio are brand names for naloxone. Doctors, emergency medical technicians, and police use naloxone to save lives when overdoses occur. It can be administered as a nasal spray or as an injection. In some states, non-medical professionals can obtain naloxone, such as people whose family members have opioid addictions. Most non-medical professionals use the nasal spray, although the injection is faster acting. Once naloxone is in the body, it blocks the way opioids act on receptors in the brain and reverses the effects of the opioid overdose. When people overdose on opioids, their breathing slows and sometimes even stops. There is only a window of about 15 minutes before permanent brain damage can occur due to lack of oxygen. If naloxone is given in time, the person overdosing begins breathing normally again. Once the crisis of the overdose has passed, it is important for the person who overdosed to seek treatment for opioid addiction.

Treatment options for steroids are different. According to NIDA, "People who use steroids often do not seek treatment for their use, with one study reporting that 56 percent of users had never told their physician about their use."[8] As with other addictions, people abusing steroids have to reach a point where they are ready to seek help. For those who seek treatment, options can include psychotherapy, endocrine therapy to ease depression symptoms, and antidepressants. Doctors are also finding that some of the medications used to fight opioid addiction might also ease symptoms of steroid dependence.

A teen convicted on drug charges could face barriers to attending college, receiving financial aid, and finding a job.

CHAPTER SIX

ILLEGAL DRUGS

There are many drugs that fall under the umbrella of illegal drugs. Some of these include cocaine, heroin, MDMA, methamphetamine, and hallucinogens. While each of these drugs is different, all are addictive and dangerous. The main danger with illegal drugs, as with other addictive substances, is that the teenage brain is still developing. This means drug use can cause greater damage to the brains of teenagers compared with those of adults. There can also be hidden dangers with illegal drug use because unlike prescription medications, illegal drugs are not regulated by the government. The people using illegal drugs never really know what they are getting. Street drugs can be laced with other dangerous or deadly substances. The consequences of illegal-drug addiction can be long-term and even deadly. Even experimenting with illegal drugs can have severe consequences for teenagers. The US Supreme Court ruled in 2002 that schools can conduct random drug tests for middle and high school students in competitive extracurricular activities, such as sports. A positive drug test can result in a lost opportunity to compete in school activities or work a part-time job. A young person caught using or selling drugs, or even being with other people who have drugs, can end up with a criminal record and the possibility of time in jail or prison.

COCAINE

Cocaine is a powerfully addictive stimulant that comes from the South American coca plant. In the late 1800s, before people realized how addictive it was, cocaine was used in medicines that treated a variety of illnesses. Advertisements said it could "restore health and vitality."[1] When introduced in 1886, Coca-Cola contained cocaine.

Cocaine is made in laboratories near the areas where it is grown in South America. In the laboratory, coca leaves are soaked in gasoline or other chemicals to remove the coca base from the coca leaves. That base is then poured into molds shaped like bricks. The liquid is squeezed out of the mixture, resulting in a hard brick that is about 50 percent cocaine.

Cocaine is sold as a white crystalline powder. Sometimes drug dealers "cut" or dilute the powder with substances such as cornstarch, flour, or baking soda so they can make more money selling less actual cocaine. Cocaine's street names include "coke," "C," "snow," "powder," and "blow." When cocaine is combined with heroin, it is called "speedball." Users inject or snort the powder form of cocaine. Cocaine is also used in a purer form called freebase. The street name "crack" is used for freebase cocaine, which is heated into liquid form and then smoked. It is called crack because when smoked, it makes a crackling sound.

Cocaine use results in short-term feelings of alertness and extra energy. Users describe pleasurable feelings of confidence and excitement. However, cocaine use also causes restlessness, anxiety, panic, and paranoia. It leads to violent and bizarre behavior in some people. The medical problems that occur with cocaine use can include heart attack, seizure, stroke, coma, and death. With repeated

ILLICIT VS. ILLEGAL

The words *illicit* and *illegal* are both used in connection with drug use, but there is a subtle difference in their meanings. *Illicit* refers both to illegal drugs and to any prescription drugs that are misused. *Illegal drugs* refers only to those that are prohibited by law. These include marijuana, which is illegal at the federal level.

use, cocaine changes the way a person's brain works, leading to physical addiction. People need more and more of the drug to produce the same level of pleasure they got with their initial use of cocaine. When they do not use the drug, they experience withdrawal.

OPIUM'S HISTORY

The earliest records referring to opium date back to 3,400 BCE from civilizations living in modern-day Southwest Asia. The early Sumerians called the opium poppy plant the "joy plant." Ancient Greek and Roman doctors used opium as a pain reliever and a sleep aid. Opium spread from this region along the Silk Road, a series of trade routes that connected China and Europe. Opium became especially prevalent in China in the 1800s. Great Britain smuggled Indian opium into China, leading to widespread addiction. Chinese people who immigrated to the United States in the 1800s brought opium with them. Heroin was first produced in 1874. By 1924, federal law made the use of heroin illegal. Today, the opium poppy grows in warm, dry climates. It is found in Turkey, Pakistan, Burma, Colombia, and Mexico.

HEROIN

Heroin is an illegal opioid drug that is highly addictive. Both heroin and prescription opioids belong to the opioid class of drugs. But prescription opioids are strictly regulated and prescribed by doctors for pain management purposes, while heroin is an illegal drug. Heroin can cause nausea, drowsiness, liver and kidney disease, mental disorders, constipation, and slowed breathing.

Slowed breathing prevents oxygen from reaching the brain and other organs and can lead to organ damage or death.

Heroin use can also cause vomiting, severe itching, and confused mental functioning. With repeated heroin use, a person may experience collapsed veins from injecting the drug, abscesses, infection in the heart, liver and kidney disease, lung disease, mental disorders, and sexual dysfunction. A person can overdose on heroin, leading to coma and permanent brain damage or death.

Heroin is made from morphine, a substance that is taken from poppy plants. Drug dealers generally sell heroin as a white or brownish powder that is diluted with other products, such as sugar, starch, or powdered milk, so they can make more money selling less actual heroin. People use heroin by injecting it, snorting it, or smoking it.

DRUG OVERDOSE DEATHS

The CDC tracks drug overdose deaths across the United States. Based on 2018 survey results, the CDC listed West Virginia, Delaware, Maryland, Pennsylvania, Ohio, and New Hampshire as having the highest rates of death caused by drug overdose. The majority of these deaths were caused by opioids, including prescription pain medicines and heroin.

"I was in active addiction since I was 13. I started doing heroin and continued using until I was 33," said Gina, who is now in recovery. "[Addiction is] the only disease that convinces you that you don't have a disease. It's cunning, baffling, and powerful."[3] Heroin use among teenagers is relatively low. Use among high school students has been generally declining since around 2000.

MDMA is often sold as a colorful pill.

MDMA

MDMA is the short name for a human-made drug called 3,4-methylenedioxymethamphetamine. MDMA was first used in the 1980s in all-night parties called raves. Its street names are "molly," "ecstasy," "E," and "X." NIDA reports that research does not yet give a clear answer to whether MDMA is physically addictive. Some people continue to use the drug in spite of negative consequences, which is a symptom of addiction. Some MDMA users also experience withdrawal and cravings if they try to stop using the drug, although researchers suggest that this may be due to psychological dependence.

MDMA use can cause depression, heart disease, impulsive behavior, lack of concentration, aggression, and anxiety. Researchers have found that people who use MDMA are more likely to engage in risky sexual behaviors. These include having sex without protection or having multiple sexual partners. The 2019 MTF survey showed that MDMA use among teenagers declined from 2014 through 2019.

METHAMPHETAMINE

Methamphetamine, or meth, is a highly addictive stimulant that affects a person's nervous system. NIDA reports that this drug contributes to violent crime more than any other. When methamphetamine is abused, the consequences are devastating for both the person and the community. Meth, a white crystal powder, can be smoked, snorted, injected, or taken by mouth. The street names for meth are "blue ice" and "crystal." Most of the meth entering the United States comes from criminal organizations operating in Mexico. Meth is usually smuggled into the United States in a liquid or powder form. Then people working in illegal laboratories convert it into crystal methamphetamine.

Methamphetamine use can cause anxiety, confusion, hallucinations, memory loss, and violent behavior. Sometimes psychotic symptoms can last for years after a person stops using the drug. Meth changes a person's brain, affecting the areas associated with emotions and cognitive function. People can also experience severe tooth decay, weight loss, and skin sores from long-term meth use. Christine Suhan, who is now in recovery, described the effects of her addiction to the Recovery Village. She said, "I once spent an entire day crouched down on my bedroom floor holding a flashlight and picking through my carpet. An entire day. I can't even tell you how many little rocks, crumbs, pieces of dirt, and granules of salt I ate hoping to find the specks of crystal meth I was convinced I had dropped the night before."[4]

METH AND SUDAFED

Methamphetamine can be made using the drug pseudoephedrine, which is contained in the decongestant Sudafed. Sudafed is designed to dry up the sniffles when a person has a cold or allergies, and it is a safe medicine when properly used. It was available over the counter at pharmacies. But drug dealer chemists learned how to misuse Sudafed to make methamphetamine. In 2005, the federal government put controls on how Sudafed could be sold to stop the abuse. Pharmacies are required to keep Sudafed behind the counter, and customers must present photo identification when they buy it. There are also limits placed on how much a person can purchase in a one-month period.

People who make meth use highly flammable household chemicals. It is common for meth labs to catch fire or explode.

Meth use among adults is a major health concern. The CDC reports that from 2015 to 2018, approximately 1.6 million adults had used meth during the past year.[5] But the 2019 MTF survey showed that methamphetamine use among teens is at a low point.

HALLUCINOGENS

According to NIDA, "Hallucinogens are a diverse group of drugs that alter a person's awareness of their surroundings as well as their own thoughts and feelings."[6] They make people sense and see things that appear real but are not. Hallucinogenic drugs can be extracted from mushrooms containing psilocybin or plants, or they can be made by humans. Hallucinogenic drugs are divided into two categories: classic hallucinogens and dissociative drugs. LSD (lysergic acid diethylamide) is a classic hallucinogen and one of the most powerful mind-altering chemicals. Its street names are "acid," "blotter acid," "dots," and "mellow yellow."

PCP (phencyclidine) is a dissociative drug. Dissociative drugs cause hallucinations and make people feel out of control, as if disconnected from their bodies. PCP's street names are "angel dust," "hog," "love boat," and "peace pill." Other hallucinogenic drugs include peyote (mescaline), DMT, ketamine, DXM, and salvia.

VIRAL HEPATITIS

Substance abuse can have many negative effects on a person's health. One significant health problem caused by drug use is viral hepatitis. This disease is an inflammation of the liver that can lead to liver cirrhosis and cancer. People increase their risk of getting viral hepatitis in two ways. Some drug users share needles and other drug equipment. Because the virus is transmitted by way of blood and other body fluids, this sharing can spread the virus. Another way viral hepatitis spreads is through unprotected sex. People abusing substances often engage in risky behaviors, such as unsafe sex.

All hallucinogens are dangerous drugs. Classic hallucinogens such as LSD cause a variety of mental problems, including mood changes, confused thinking, paranoia, visual disturbances, and bizarre behavior. Dissociative drugs such as PCP can cause speech problems, anxiety, hallucinations, memory loss, seizures, depression, and thoughts of suicide.

Since the MTF survey began tracking teenagers' drug use in 1975, less than 10 percent of twelfth graders have reported using LSD or other hallucinogens in the year before they took the survey. Across the years, there have been some small rises and drops in use, but hallucinogen use remained under 10 percent from 1975 to around 2001. Since that time, the use of LSD and other hallucinogens among twelfth graders has remained less than 6 percent.[7]

TREATMENT

There are no FDA-approved medications to treat cocaine, MDMA, methamphetamine, and hallucinogen addictions, but researchers are working on medications. For cocaine abuse, researchers are working on a vaccine that could help lessen the risk of relapse once a person has stopped using cocaine. According to NIDA, "The vaccine stimulates the immune system to create cocaine-specific antibodies that bind to cocaine, preventing it from getting into the brain."[8] There are, however, FDA-approved medicines that can help people overcome heroin addiction. These are the same medicines—buprenorphine, methadone, and naltrexone—that have proven to be effective in fighting prescription drug opioid addiction. Even though there are no FDA-approved medications for hallucinogen abuse, doctors can use medicines to treat the anxiety and depression that often accompanies withdrawal from hallucinogens.

Several European countries are home to drug-consumption rooms. These facilities provide pure drugs and clean needles to drug users to help prevent the

Drug-consumption rooms help reduce rates of fatal overdose by providing medical care to the people who use the rooms.

adverse effects of sharing needles and using drugs laced with other products. The facilities also provide counseling, as well as medical care in case of an overdose. The goal of these facilities is to reduce public drug use and provide more accessible addiction treatment. They also reduce rates of drug-related death.

A variety of behavioral treatments can be successfully used to treat people who are addicted to illegal drugs. Two of the most common are CBT and contingency management therapy. They have both proven to be effective for treating cocaine, heroin, and methamphetamine addiction. CBT helps patients recognize the situations where they might be most likely to use these drugs and then avoid those situations. In the case of heroin, these behavioral treatments are especially effective when used alongside the medications available to treat the addiction. Patients have the most success fighting methamphetamine addiction using behavioral therapies that combine family education, counseling, recovery support groups, and drug testing. For MDMA addiction and hallucinogenic drugs, CBT has proven to be the most effective treatment. Taking part in recovery groups along with CBT can be especially effective in overcoming addiction. Support groups can be invaluable to people working to overcome addiction to illegal drugs.

Kratom, which comes from a tropical plant, is one of many dangerous drugs that is not illegal in the United States.

CHAPTER SEVEN

LESSER-KNOWN DRUGS

Drugs such as marijuana, cocaine, or heroin might sound familiar to most people. But there are a number of lesser-known drugs that are frequently abused. These lesser-known drugs can still have harmful and even deadly consequences when a person abuses them. Kratom, bath salts, synthetic cannabinoids, and inhalants are some of these dangerous drugs.

KRATOM

Kratom is a tropical plant that grows in Southeast Asia. Some people assume because it is a plant, it is safe to use. But kratom is extremely dangerous. David Seitz, medical director of the rehab program Ascendant, said, "I think the major challenge is a perceptual one. . . . [Young people] don't consider it a drug until they get into trouble with it."[1]

The Kratom plant's leaves contain ingredients that have a psychotropic effect on humans. People take kratom as a pill, capsule, gum, or extract. Its street names include "biak," "ketum," "kakuam," "ithang," and "thom." Taken in small amounts, kratom causes increased energy,

alertness, and sociability, but it can be addictive. There are
no federal laws making kratom illegal. However, some cities
and states have banned it, and the US Drug Enforcement
Administration (DEA) has listed kratom as a "Drug and
Chemical of Concern." The FDA has not approved kratom
for any use and has issued warnings against people using
it. Between 2011 and 2017, poison-control centers in the
United States received about 1,800 reports involving the
use of kratom.[2] About half of these resulted in serious
health problems such as seizures and high blood pressure.
Some of these calls resulted in death.

Kratom affects a person's brain in similar ways to opioids and stimulants. It can lead to dangerous side effects such as loss of appetite, weight loss, insomnia, liver-related illnesses, and even psychotic symptoms. Sometimes kratom is packaged as a dietary supplement and laced with other ingredients, although it cannot be legally marketed in the United States as a dietary supplement. These versions of kratom have caused people's deaths.

BATH SALTS

Bath salts, also called synthetic cathinone, have nothing to do with the colorful bath bombs that can be purchased at a drug store. Cathinone is a substance found in the khat plant, which grows in Africa and Arabia. Bath salts are human-made drugs that are chemically similar to the cathinone in the khat plant. But according to NIDA, "Human-made versions of cathinone can be much stronger than the natural product and, in some cases, very dangerous."[4]

People take bath salts by swallowing, snorting, smoking, or injecting them. The street names include "bliss," "cloud nine," "lunar wave," "vanilla sky," and "white lightning." Bath salts can cause dangerous symptoms such as paranoia, hallucinations, and even death. Bath salts

DANGEROUS, BUT NOT ILLEGAL

Some powerful, dangerous drugs are illegal while others are not. So why aren't all dangerous drugs outlawed? One reason is that human-made drugs, such as bath salts, can be easily changed. The drug makers constantly change minor ingredients in the drug. If lawmakers attempt to outlaw the drug, drug makers simply tweak the formula just a little and reintroduce it as a new drug. By doing this, they are constantly dodging the efforts of law enforcement to shut down the production of these dangerous drugs.

HISTORY OF BATH SALTS

Bath salts are a designer drug, meaning they are made in a lab. The drug first appeared in France in the 1920s. But then it seemed to disappear for many decades. The drug reemerged in 2004 when someone published a recipe for making it on the internet, and the drug gained sudden popularity across Europe. By 2010, bath salts had become widely used in British nightclubs and were soon as popular as cocaine. Bath salts gained widespread use among American drug users around 2011. Bizarre incidents ensued. One 21-year-old man saw throngs of police cars where there were none after taking bath salts. The effects of the drug lasted for days. He was hospitalized and later died by suicide. Another person left her two-year-old child on the highway. By mid-2011, bath salts were banned in 28 states, and they were banned federally in 2012.

affect a person's brain and can be addictive. People sometimes choose to use bath salts as a cheap substitute for cocaine or methamphetamine. While many drugs used in bath salts have been banned at the federal level, it is difficult to enforce this ban. People who sell these drugs often label them "not for human consumption" and advertise them as plant food to work around federal regulations.

A 2015 study published in the *American Journal on Addictions* showed that approximately 1 percent of high school seniors had tried bath salts during the past year. Of those who tried the drug, almost one-fifth of them reported using bath salts 40 times

Bath salts were named for their resemblance to Epsom salts in an attempt to disguise their true use, but they are not the same.

or more.[5] The study also found that most bath salts users had used alcohol, marijuana, or other drugs as well.

Abusing bath salts can cause paranoia, hallucinations, panic attacks, violent behavior, chest pain, dehydration, kidney failure, and even death. News reports have told stories of people who act out with violent, bizarre behavior after using bath salts. This drug affects the body like cocaine does, but in more powerful ways. In a 2012 research study, scientists tested rats and found that bath salts are at least ten times more potent than cocaine in the ways they affected the rats' motor activity and heart function.

SYNTHETIC CANNABINOIDS

Synthetic cannabinoids are addictive, mind-altering drugs that contain chemicals called cannabinoids. These chemicals are found in marijuana plants. Synthetic cannabinoids are sometimes falsely advertised as being safe and legal alternatives to marijuana. The drug is even called fake weed or synthetic marijuana. But synthetic cannabinoids are actually more unpredictable and have a more powerful impact on the human brain than marijuana. They can also be life-threatening. Synthetic cannabinoids are usually smoked, but they can also be brewed as tea. The drug's street names are "K2," "spice," "joker," "black mamba," "Kush," and "Kronic."

Synthetic cannabinoids are not just a single drug but rather hundreds of different synthetic cannabinoid chemicals. This makes them challenging to regulate. The federal government has declared many of the specific chemicals illegal. Some states have also passed laws making synthetic cannabinoids illegal. Yet people who

K2 is one of more than one hundred different synthetic cannabinoids.

make the drugs bypass these laws by creating new products using slightly different chemicals, or they label their products as "not for human consumption." The 2019 MTF Survey showed a five-year decrease among tenth and twelfth graders using synthetic cannabinoids but a one-year increase by eighth graders.

Synthetic cannabinoids cause mind-altering symptoms like marijuana does, but the symptoms are more unpredictable and dangerous. These drugs can cause extreme anxiety, confusion, paranoia, hallucinations, violent behavior, and suicidal thoughts. Medical professionals are

WHY TEENS USE DRUGS

Teenagers who use drugs make the choice to do so for a variety of reasons. According to NIDA, teens choose to use drugs in order to fit in and be accepted among their peers. They use drugs in order to feel good or to feel better about stressful things happening in their lives. Some teens use drugs in order to do better in sports or academics. And some teenagers are simply experimenting, seeking new experiences or thrills. In an article for Psychology Today, David Sack wrote, "The problem is we don't know in advance who will become addicted, to which type of drug, and at what level of use. Occasional use of any drug can quickly lead to addiction for someone who has a personal or family history of addiction or mental illness, difficulty coping with stress, strained family ties, or other risk factors for addiction."[7]

seeing an increasing number of deaths related to synthetic cannabinoid use.

INHALANTS

Inhalants are substances that a person abuses by inhaling the vapors. They include products such as solvents, aerosol sprays, gases, or nitrites. Inhalants are usually easy to find around the home in items such as spray paints, markers, hair spray, cleaning products, or glue. People abuse them by breathing the fumes. This is often referred to as "huffing." Inhalants have mind-altering properties that cause slurred speech, lack of coordination, dizziness, and a high feeling. People often do not consider these products to be drugs because they have useful purposes around the home. But their ability to be

Aerosol items such as spray paint and hair spray can be misused as inhalants.

misused classifies them as drugs. Inhalants are not usually addictive, although a person can develop substance use disorder from using them repeatedly. Inhalants are typically used by children and teenagers because they are easy to obtain. They are the only substances used more by younger teens than older teens.

People who use inhalants experience slurred speech, lack of control of body movement, dizziness, nosebleeds, and a feeling of being high. Over time, people who use inhalants can experience damage to the liver, kidneys, bone marrow, nerves, and brain. Inhalants can cause seizures, coma, and even death.

TREATMENT

NIDA reports that there are no specific medical treatments available for kratom addiction. Behavioral therapy seems to help some people seeking treatment. However, scientists are still working to determine therapies or medicines that might be effective. There are also no FDA-approved medications to treat the withdrawal symptoms from bath salts. The suggested treatment for a person who wants to stop using bath salts usually includes behavioral therapy. Contingency management therapy has proven successful as a treatment for inhalant use. Behavioral therapies and medications have not been tested specifically for their

GATEWAY DRUGS

A gateway drug is a drug that a person might use before moving on to more dangerous drugs. For example, some people think of marijuana, alcohol, or tobacco as gateway drugs to other drug use. Some research does connect marijuana use to substance use disorders involving harder drugs. Among high school students, research supports the idea that alcohol is a gateway drug that leads to the use of tobacco, marijuana, and other substances. However, NIDA reports that other explanations exist: "An alternative to the gateway-drug hypothesis is that people who are more vulnerable to drug-taking are simply more likely to start with readily available substances such as marijuana, tobacco, or alcohol, and their subsequent social interactions with others who use drugs increases their chances of trying other drugs."[8]

Contingency management therapy rewards patients for remaining drug-free with prizes such as gift cards or cash.

usefulness in treating synthetic cannabinoids addiction. However, NIDA does recommend that health-care providers screen any patients using synthetic cannabinoids to see whether they might also have mental health conditions. Treating the mental health conditions can help a person to better fight the substance addiction.

Support groups, such as 12-step groups or group therapy, can be a vital part of treatment for substance addiction.

TREATING SUBSTANCE ADDICTION

Substance addiction is a costly problem in terms of its effects on people who use drugs, their families, and their communities. The health consequences of substance addiction are dangerous and sometimes deadly. But the good news is that there is hope. People have been successful in overcoming substance addiction and moving forward as productive members of their families and communities. Musician Eric Clapton has been sober for more than two decades, following addiction to heroin, cocaine, and alcohol. Clapton says, "My identity shifted when I got into recovery. That's who I am now, and it actually gives me greater pleasure to have that identity than to be a musician or anything else, because it keeps me in a manageable size."[1]

SUCCESS IN TREATING DRUG ADDICTION

There is a treatment gap in the United States. The 2013 NSDUH showed that approximately 22.7 million Americans needed treatment for a substance abuse problem related to alcohol or drugs, but only about 2.5 million people received treatment at a facility.[2] Many people who need help for substance addiction are not getting it. There is room for improvement in making help available for those battling addiction.

The good news for people struggling with addiction is that most people who get into treatment and stay in treatment will stop using drugs, according to NIDA. The people who stay in treatment also improve the way they function socially, psychologically, and at work. The people who are successful in treatment also are less likely to be involved in criminal activity in the future. Yet NIDA also notes that the success of treatment for drug addiction varies from person to person. Its success or lack of success depends on factors such as people's specific problems and the treatment they choose to tackle their problems.

HOW TO VIEW SUCCESS IN TREATMENT

Medical professionals suggest that viewing drug addiction treatment as either a success or failure is not the best way to look at it. They recommend that drug addiction treatment be viewed more like other chronic diseases that are managed successfully over time without necessarily being cured. For example, people who are treated for diabetes, asthma, or hypertension might see their symptoms decrease,

TWELVE-STEP PROGRAMS

Twelve-step programs have proven to be successful tools in treating addiction. Twelve-step programs involve self-help meetings where group members talk about past mistakes and encourage one another to stay sober. Many professional treatment programs encourage their patients to connect with a 12-step group as part of their ongoing goal of sober living. Alcoholics Anonymous (AA) is the most well-known of these programs. A 2020 study at Stanford School of Medicine reported that many people have found AA to be an effective path to sobriety.

There are even 12-step groups for people who are affected by a family member's addiction. Al-Anon is for families who are struggling to cope with a family member's addiction. Alateen is a similar group specifically for teens.

The Substance Abuse and Mental Health Service Administration (SAMHSA) helps connect people to treatment facilities and support groups. The free, 24-hour SAMHSA number is 1-800-662-HELP (4357).

WHAT IS AN INTERVENTION?

Sometimes a person suffering from drug or alcohol addiction is unable or unwilling to seek help for themselves. This is when family members and close friends can step in by staging an intervention. An intervention is a planned gathering where family members and friends confront the person about his or her addiction and urge the person to seek help. Family or friends often enlist the help of a professional such as a doctor, licensed drug or alcohol counselor, or interventionist. During the intervention, family and friends confront the person with examples of destructive behavior and talk about the ways it is affecting family and friends. They present a treatment plan, laying out goals and guidelines for working together to encourage the person to enter a treatment program.

and if so, the treatment is called a success. If their symptoms increase again later, it is not viewed as a failure. Instead, the doctors realize they need to adjust the treatment in some way. The diseases are managed so the person can live a healthier life. Health-care professionals recommend that addiction treatment be viewed in the same way. People may relapse to drug abuse after initial success in treatment. What is needed then is an adjustment to the treatment approach so that people's healthy lifestyles can be managed and maintained over a long period of time. Bill, a military veteran, described his road to recovery: "I've been in recovery for 23 years, and I've

Professionals urge people seeking treatment for addiction not to view recovery in strict terms of success and failure.

relapsed seven times. But, the support I get in the recovery community has helped me every time I start drinking again. No judgment, just help and support. Without my recovery program, I know I would have drank myself into an early grave every time. Recovery isn't always easy, but it certainly beats the alternative."[4]

Substance addiction affects people's behavior and how their brains function. These effects are amplified in teenagers, whose brains are still developing. The changes in the brain can last even after the person has stopped using drugs. It is not surprising that people who have initial success in drug treatment may sometimes return to abusing drugs. Finding the right treatment, whether inpatient or outpatient, and staying in treatment for the right amount of time are both key to a person's success in overcoming substance addiction. Research shows that most people struggling with substance addiction need at least three months in drug treatment for the best chances of long-term success. For teenagers, long-term inpatient treatment provides other services too, such as family therapy and schooling.

In general, behavioral therapies are the most common treatment for substance addiction. These therapies often include a combination of individual, family, and group counseling. Through these therapies, a person learns strategies and problem-solving skills for withstanding the

Some addictions can be helped with medication.

temptation of drug abuse. Medications designed to combat substance addiction can be useful too. The most effective treatments for substance addiction typically combine behavioral therapies and medications.

INNOVATIONS IN TREATMENT

Beyond the existing treatments for substance addiction, researchers are looking for new ways to fight this problem. Scientists are studying the changes that occur

ADDICTION SCIENCE AWARD

Some science-savvy teens are taking the lead in advancing the study of addiction. They are creating science projects and competing for the annual Addiction Science Award. This award is part of the International Science and Engineering Fair, the largest high school science competition.

In the 2019 competition, Aditya Tummala won first prize by developing a tamper-resistant opioid. An opioid pill that can be easily tampered with can be easily abused. Aditya, a high school freshman from South Dakota, made a gummy substance that is mixed with the opioid. The substance prevents the pill from being crushed or melted, meaning it cannot be snorted or injected. Tamper-resistant medicines are just one research area where scientists are working to combat drug abuse.

in the human brain when a person uses drugs. Having a better understanding of what happens to the communication routes in the brain because of drug use can help scientists find better ways to treat addiction.

One branch of addiction research involves studying people's genes to determine whether they have genetic predispositions to becoming addicted or engaging in addictive behaviors. This test is called the Genetic Addiction Risk Score. Doctors can take a cheek swab from a person and then analyze it to identify the person's risk for addiction. After being tested, people whose tests show vulnerability

Learning how to treat pain without the use of opioids can help solve the opioid crisis.

to addiction can make different choices, including the decision to never use addictive substances.

The US government's National Institutes of Health (NIH) is also working to apply science to the problem of addiction. The NIH Helping to End Addiction Long-Term (HEAL) Initiative is funding research projects to attack the opioid-abuse public health problem. Its research is focused on gaining a better understanding of pain and how to treat it, along with improving the treatment available for people addicted to opioids.

HEALTHY LIVING FREE FROM ADDICTION

Substance addiction is a major health crisis affecting teenagers, their families, and their communities. Substance abuse leads to significant health problems, including mental disorders, chronic diseases, overdoses, and death. Millions of people in the United States use illegal drugs in ways that affect their health and cause problems in their work, family life, and communities. With almost half of twelfth graders in the United States reporting that they used an illicit drug in 2019, a significant number of teenagers are at risk for the long-term health problems and other challenges that come with substance abuse.

"I used to picture an addict as someone under a bridge with a needle in his arm," says Abbey Zorzi, who started abusing prescription drugs before moving on to using heroin. "The end of addiction might look that way, but it sure doesn't begin like that. I never pictured myself as a drug addict until I became one as a teenager. . . . Once that drug was in me, it told me what to do. I didn't take heroin; heroin took me." As a college freshman, Zorzi entered a month-long treatment program. Today, she says, "It *is* possible to recover. Any addict can stop using, lose the desire to use, and find a new way of life."[6]

The best way to avoid the problems of substance addiction is to never start using substances that lead to addiction. Teenagers can explore and enjoy the world that is opening up in front of them in so many ways that do not include experimenting with addictive substances. They can support and encourage their friends in making choices that build healthy living habits. For the person who is already struggling with substance abuse or addiction, there is hope, and help is available. Treatment can lead to sober living, far from the dangerous and deadly influences of substance addiction.

SOBER LIVING HOMES

Sober living homes are places for adults recovering from drug addiction to live. They are sometimes called halfway houses or recovery houses. Residents living in these homes take part in 12-step recovery programs to help them toward their goal of sober living. According to Douglas L. Polcin, a researcher studying these homes, "Destructive living environments can derail recovery for even highly motivated individuals."[7] These homes often offer people a safe place to live when they are moving out of a drug treatment program and before they move back to their own homes. Research reveals that sober living homes are helpful for people recovering from drug addiction. The people in sober living homes showed improvement in their use of drugs and alcohol, their employment, their psychiatric symptoms, and their arrests.

FACTS ABOUT SUBSTANCE ADDICTION

- Substance addiction is a brain disorder in which repeated substance use changes a person's brain over time. This is especially dangerous for teenagers, whose brains are still developing.

- People who are addicted to substances keep using them and feel powerless to stop, even though the substances cause problems with their health, relationships, and school or work.

IMPACT ON DAILY LIFE

- In 2019, the University of Michigan's Monitoring the Future survey showed that about half of all twelfth graders in the United States reported that they had used illicit drugs at some point in their life.

- Substance addiction leads to risky behavior and severe health consequences, including heart attack, stroke, and death.

DEALING WITH SUBSTANCE ADDICTION

- People can be successful in overcoming substance addiction, usually through a combination of behavioral therapy and medications targeted at dealing with the addiction.

- Twelve-step groups such as Alcoholics Anonymous are available across the country for teenagers and adults struggling with substance addictions. They are proven to be useful in helping a person achieve sober living.

QUOTE

"We have to recognize (addiction) isn't evidence of a character flaw or a moral failing. It's a chronic disease of the brain that deserves the same compassion that any other chronic illness does, like diabetes or heart disease."

—Dr. Vivek Murthy, US surgeon general from 2014 to 2017

GLOSSARY

abscess

A sore, swollen area on the body where pus
is present.

aerosol

Relating to substances in spray cans that are released
by pushing a button; also refers to a thin cloud of
these substances in the air.

cognitive

Related to the act or process of thinking, reasoning,
remembering, imagining, or learning.

compulsive

Having powerful urges to do something.

depressant

A substance that affects a person's central nervous
system by slowing down brain function.

diabetes

A disease in which a person's body doesn't properly
process sugar.

endocrine
Related to the system of glands in the body that makes hormones for growth and proper function.

genetic
Having to do with the combination of traits that parents pass on to their children.

HIV/AIDS
A virus and resulting disease that attacks the body's ability to fight infections; often spread by shared needles or unprotected sex.

relapse
To fall or slip back into a former practice.

stimulant
A substance that affects a person's central nervous system by speeding up its activity.

synthetic
Made by humans.

ADDITIONAL RESOURCES

SELECTED BIBLIOGRAPHY

"Drugs, Brains, and Behavior: The Science of Addiction." *National Institute on Drug Abuse*, July 2018, drugabuse.gov. Accessed 19 May 2020.

"Know the Risks of Marijuana." *Substance Abuse and Mental Health Services Administration*, 26 Sept. 2019, samhsa.gov. Accessed 19 May 2020.

McMinn, Sean. "More Teens than Ever Are Vaping. Here's What We Know about Their Habits." *NPR*, 6 Nov. 2019, npr.org. Accessed 19 May 2020.

FURTHER READINGS

Allen, John. *The Opioid Crisis*. ReferencePoint, 2020.

Amstutz, Lisa J. *Alcohol*. Abdo, 2019.

Hand, Carol. *Tobacco*. Abdo, 2019.

ONLINE RESOURCES

To learn more about substance addiction, please visit **abdobooklinks.com** or scan this QR code. These links are routinely monitored and updated to provide the most current information available.

MORE INFORMATION

For more information on this subject, contact or visit the following organizations:

Alateen

1600 Corporate Landing Pkwy.
Virginia Beach, VA 23454
888-4AL-ANON (888-425-2666)
al-anon.org

Alateen, a part of Al-Anon, offers a place where teens can find effective ways to cope with the problems that come from someone else's alcoholism.

National Institute on Drug Abuse (NIDA)

6001 Executive Blvd.
Room 5213, MSC 9561
Bethesda, MD 20892
301-443-1124
teens.drugabuse.gov

The National Institute on Drug Abuse (NIDA) is part of the National Institutes of Health, the US government's medical research agency. NIDA provides facts about drugs and how they affect a person's brain and body. NIDA for Teens is a website with videos, games, and more to teach teens about drug addiction.

SOURCE NOTES

CHAPTER 1. THE CHALLENGES OF SUBSTANCE ADDICTION

1. "The Science of Drug Use and Addiction: The Basics." *NIDA*, July 2018, drugabuse.gov. Accessed 28 July 2020.

2. A. Thomas McLellan. "Substance Misuse and Substance Use Disorders." *Transactions of the American Clinical and Climatological Association*, 2017, ncbi.nlm.nih.gov. Accessed 28 July 2020.

3. "The Science of Drug Use and Addiction."

4. William R. Kelly. "The Drug Problem in the US Is Not What We Think It Is." *Psychology Today*, 26 Sept. 2018, psychologytoday.com. Accessed 28 July 2020.

5. Kelly, "The Drug Problem in the US."

6. "2017 Results." *High School YRBS*, n.d., cdc.gov. Accessed 7 Aug. 2020.

7. Kelly, "The Drug Problem in the US."

8. "Substance Addiction." *Harvard*, Dec. 2014, health.harvard.edu. Accessed 28 July 2020.

9. Josh Hafner. "1 in 7 in USA Will Face Substance Addiction." *USA Today*, 17 Nov. 2016, usatoday.com. Accessed 28 July 2020.

CHAPTER 2. ALCOHOL

1. "Alcoholism." *Holyoke*, 2020, mtholyoke.edu. Accessed 28 July 2020.

2. "Age 21 Minimum Legal Drinking Age." *CDC*, 7 Jan. 2020, cdc.gov. Accessed 7 Aug. 2020.

3. Lloyd D. Johnston et al. "Key Findings on Adolescent Drug Use." *MTF*, Jan. 2020, monitoringthefuture.org. Accessed 28 July 2020.

4. Johnston et al., "Key Findings on Adolescent Drug Use."

5. "Alcohol Facts and Statistics." *NIH*, Feb. 2020, niaaa.nih.gov. Accessed 7 Aug. 2020.

6. "Alcohol Facts and Statistics."

7. "Alcohol Use." *CDC*, 30 Dec. 2019, cdc.gov. Accessed 28 July 2020.

8. Michael King. "My Addiction Recovery Story." *AES*, 2018, addictioneducationsociety.org. Accessed 28 July 2020.

9. Serena Gordon. "Millions Hurt by 'Secondhand' Alcohol." *WebMD*, 2 July 2019, webmd.com. Accessed 28 July 2020.

10. "Alcohol Use Disorder (AUD)." *Medline Plus*, 29 Apr. 2020, medlineplus.gov. Accessed 28 July 2020.

11. "Alcohol Facts and Statistics."

12. Raychelle Cassada Lohmann. "Teen Binge Drinking." *Psychology Today*, 26 Jan. 2013, psychologytoday.com. Accessed 28 July 2020.

CHAPTER 3. TOBACCO AND NICOTINE

1. "Know the Risks." *Smokefree Teen*, n.d., teen.smokefree.gov. Accessed 23 June 2020.

2. Kathleen Raven. "Teen Vaping Linked to More Health Risks." *Yale Medicine*, 18 Dec. 2019, yalemedicine.org. Accessed 28 July 2020.

3. "Find Help: ATOD." *SAMHSA*, 2020, samhsa.gov. Accessed 7 Aug. 2020.

4. Sean McMinn. "More Teens Than Ever Are Vaping." *NPR*, 6 Nov. 2019, npr.org. Accessed 7 Aug. 2020.

5. "Find Help: ATOD."

6. "Find Help: ATOD."

7. "Economic Trends in Tobacco." *CDC*, 18 May 2020, cdc.gov. Accessed 7 Aug. 2020.

8. J. Taylor Hays. "What Is Thirdhand Smoke, and Why Is It a Concern?" *Mayo Clinic*, 13 July 2017, mayoclinic.org. Accessed 28 July 2020.

9. "Smoking 'Causes Damage in Minutes,' US Experts Claim." *BBC News*, 16 Jan. 2011, bbc.com. Accessed 28 July 2020.

10. "The Problem(s) with Nicotine." *NIDA*, 24 June 2019, teens.drugabuse.gov. Accessed 28 July 2020.

11. "Health Effects of Secondhand Smoke." *CDC*, 27 Feb. 2020, cdc.gov. Accessed 28 July 2020.

CHAPTER 4. MARIJUANA

1. Emily Sohn. "Weighing the Dangers of Cannabis." *Nature*, 28 Aug. 2019, nature.com. Accessed 28 July 2020.

2. "Find Help: ATOD." *SAMHSA*, 2020, samhsa.gov. Accessed 7 Aug. 2020.

3. R. Sam Barclay. "Marijuana Can Be Addictive." *Healthline*, 2 Aug. 2019, healthline.com. Accessed 28 July 2020.

4. Agata Blaszczak-Boxe. "7 Ways Marijuana May Affect the Brain." *Live Science*, 1 July 2016, livescience.com. Accessed 28 July 2020.

5. "Map of Marijuana Legality by State." *DISA Global Solutions*, July 2020, disa.com. Accessed 28 July 2020.

6. Katie Hunt. "Single Joint Linked with Temporary Psychiatric Symptoms, Review Finds," *CNN*, 17 Mar. 2020, cnn.com. Accessed 28 July 2020.

7. Blaszczak-Boxe, "7 Ways Marijuana May Affect the Brain."

CHAPTER 5. PRESCRIPTION DRUGS

1. "Cortney." *CDC*, 22 Sept. 2017, cdc.gov. Accessed 28 July 2020.

2. F. Leland McClure. "The Prescription Drug Misuse Epidemic?" *OHS*, 1 Sept. 2015, ohsonline.com. Accessed 28 July 2020.

3. "Rise in Prescription Drug Misuse and Abuse Impacting Teens." *SAMHSA*, 22 July 2020, samhsa.gov. Accessed 28 July 2020.

4. Andis Robeznieks. "5 Tips for Safely Storing Opioids at Home." *AMA*, 6 Sept. 2018, ama-assn.org. Accessed 28 July 2020.

5. Lasherica Thornton. "Comic Book Educates Teens." *Jackson Sun*, 18 Feb. 2020, jacksonsun.com. Accessed 28 July 2020.

6. "Opioid Overdose Crisis." *NIDA*, 27 May 2020, drugabuse.gov. Accessed 28 July 2020.

7. "Are Some Babies Born Addicted?" *NIDA*, 24 Sept. 2018, teens.drugabuse.gov. Accessed 28 July 2020.

8. "What Treatments Are Effective for Anabolic Steroid Misuse?" *NIDA*, Feb. 2018, drugabuse.gov. Accessed 28 July 2020.

CHAPTER 6. ILLEGAL DRUGS

1. "Cocaine." *History*, 21 Aug. 2018, history.com. Accessed 28 July 2020.

2. "Why Do Adolescents Take Drugs?" *NIDA*, Jan. 2014, drugabuse.gov. Accessed 28 July 2020.

3. "Living Recovery." *RCA*, 2020, recoverycentersofamerica.com. Accessed 28 July 2020.

4. "Crystal Clear." *Recovery Village*, n.d., therecoveryvillage.com. Accessed 2 July 2020.

5. "Meth Use Among Adults." *CDC*, 2020, cdc.gov. Accessed 7 Aug. 2020

6. "What Are Hallucinogens?" *NIDA*, Apr. 2019, drugabuse.gov. Accessed 28 July 2020.

7. Lloyd D. Johnston et al. "Key Findings on Adolescent Drug Use." *MTF*, Jan. 2020, monitoringthefuture.org. Accessed 28 July 2020.

8. "How Is Cocaine Addiction Treated?" *NIDA*, May 2016, drugabuse.gov. Accessed 28 July 2020.

9. Michael King. "My Addiction Recovery Story." *AES*, 2018,
   addictioneducationsociety.org. Accessed 28 July 2020.

CHAPTER 7. LESSER-KNOWN DRUGS

1. Christina Frank. "Kratom: A Legal Drug that's Dangerously Addictive."
   Child Mind Institute, 2020, childmind.org. Accessed 28 July 2020.

2. "Kratom: Unsafe and Ineffective." *Mayo Clinic*, 3 June 2020,
   mayoclinic.org. Accessed 7 Aug. 2020.

3. Peter Grinspoon. "Kratom." *Harvard Health Publishing*, 26 Sept. 2019,
   health.harvard.edu. Accessed 28 July 2020.

4. "Synthetic Cathinones ('Bath Salts') DrugFacts." *NIDA*, July 2020,
   drugabuse.gov. Accessed 28 July 2020.

5. Douglas Main. "1 Percent of Teens Use Bath Salts, Survey Says."
   Newsweek, 16 July 2015, newsweek.com. Accessed 7 Aug. 2020.

6. "Synthetic Cannabinoids." *CDC*, 2018, cdc.gov. Accessed 28 July 2020.

7. David Sack. "Teen Drug Use." *Psychology Today*, 8 Oct. 2013,
   psychologytoday.com. Accessed 28 July 2020.

8. "Is Marijuana a Gateway Drug?" *NIDA*, July 2020, drugabuse.gov.
   Accessed 28 July 2020.

CHAPTER 8. TREATING SUBSTANCE ADDICTION

1. "9 Memorable Quotes from Former Addicts." *Drugabuse.com*, 2020,
   drugabuse.com. Accessed 28 July 2020.

2. "Overview of Findings from the 2013 NSDUH Report." *SAMHSA*, 4 Sept.
   2014, samhsa.gov. Accessed 7 Aug. 2020.

3. "Facing Addiction in America." *US DHHS*, 2016,
   addiction.surgeongeneral.gov. Accessed 28 July 2020.

4. "9 Memorable Quotes from Former Addicts."

5. John Giordano. "New Cutting-Edge Treatments that Are Improving
   Outcomes." *Sober World*, 1 Apr. 2019, thesoberworld.com. Accessed
   28 July 2020.

6. "Abbey Zorzi, 22." *Just Think Twice*, n.d., justthinktwice.gov. Accessed
   2 July 2020.

7. Douglas L. Polcin et al. "What Did We Learn from Our Study on
   Sober Living Houses?" *Journal of Psychoactive Drugs*, Dec. 2010,
   ncbi.nlm.nih.gov. Accessed 28 July 2020.